MURDER INC.

VOLUME ONE
VALENTINE'S TRUST

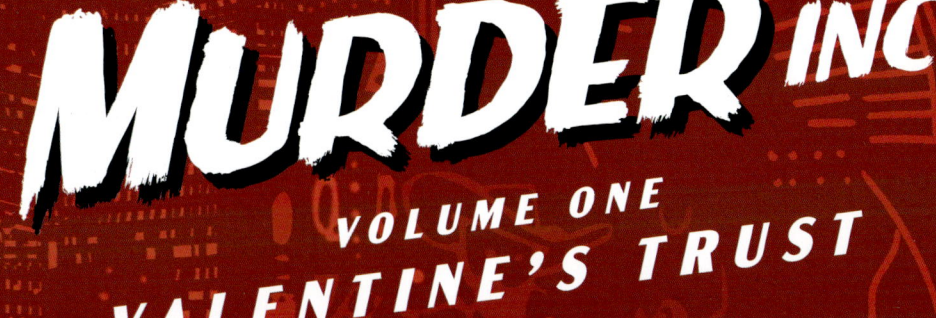

VOLUME ONE
VALENTINE'S TRUST

CREATED BY
BRIAN MICHAEL BENDIS
& MICHAEL AVON OEMING

COLORS
TAKI SOMA

LETTERS
CHRIS ELIOPOULOS

SERIES AND COLLECTION COVER ART
MICHAEL AVON OEMING

DARK HORSE BOOKS

DARK HORSE

PUBLISHER MIKE RICHARDSON **COLLECTION EDITOR** DANIEL CHABON

ASSISTANT EDITORS CHUCK HOWITT-LEASE AND MISHA GEHR

DESIGNER ETHAN KIMBERLING **DIGITAL ART TECHNICIAN** BETSY HOWITT

ORIGINAL PRINTING

PUBLISHER ALISA BENDIS **EDITOR** JENNIFER GRÜNWALD

To find a comics shop in your area, visit comicshoplocator.com.

MURDER INC. VOLUME ONE: VALENTINE'S TRUST
Copyright © 2018, 2023 Jinxworld Inc. All rights reserved. Originally published in single magazine form in *The United States of Murder Inc.* #1–#6. Copyright © 2016, 2018 Jinxworld, Inc. All Rights Reserved. Murder Inc., its logo design, the Jinxworld logo, all characters, their distinctive likenesses and related elements featured in this publication are trademarks of Jinxworld, Inc. Dark Horse Books® and the Dark Horse logo are trademarks of Dark Horse Comics LLC, registered in various categories and countries. All rights reserved. No portion of this publication may be reproduced or transmitted, in any form or by any means, without the express written permission of Dark Horse Comics LLC. Names, characters, places, and incidents featured in this publication either are the product of the author's imagination or are used fictitiously. Any resemblance to actual persons (living or dead), events, institutions, or locales, without satiric intent, is coincidental.

This volume collects *The United States of Murder Inc.* #1–#6, along with all covers and a sketchbook section.

Published by
Dark Horse Books
A division of
Dark Horse Comics LLC
10956 SE Main Street
Milwaukie, OR 97222

DarkHorse.com

First edition: January 2023
Ebook ISBN 978-1-50673-043-1
Trade paperback ISBN 978-1-50673-027-1

10 9 8 7 6 5 4 3 2 1
Printed in China

Neil Hankerson, *Executive Vice President* · Tom Weddle, *Chief Financial Officer* · Dale LaFountain, *Chief Information Officer* · Tim Wiesch, *Vice President of Licensing* · Vanessa Todd-Holmes, *Vice President of Production and Scheduling* · Mark Bernardi, *Vice President of Book Trade and Digital Sales* · Randy Lahrman, *Vice President of Product Development and Sales* · Ken Lizzi, *General Counsel* · Dave Marshall, *Editor in Chief* · Davey Estrada, *Editorial Director* · Chris Warner, *Senior Books Editor* · Cara O'Neil, *Senior Director of Marketing* · Cary Grazzini, *Director of Specialty Projects* · Lia Ribacchi, *Art Director* · Michael Gombos, *Senior Director of Licensed Publications* · Kari Yadro, *Director of Custom Programs* · Kari Torson, *Director of International Licensing* · Christina Niece, *Director of Scheduling*

Library of Congress Cataloging-in-Publication Data

Names: Bendis, Brian Michael, author. | Oeming, Michael Avon, artist. | Soma, Taki, colorist. | Eliopoulos, Chris, letterer.
Title: Valentine's trust / created by Brian Michael Bendis & Michael Avon Oeming ; colors, Taki Soma ; letters, Chris Eliopoulos.
Description: First edition. | Milwaukie, OR : Dark Horse Books, 2023. | Series: Murder Inc. ; volume one | "This volume collects The United States of Murder Inc. #1-#6, along with all covers and a sketchbook section." | Summary: "Discover a world in which the families of organized crime never lost their stranglehold on the United States. Today is the day that Valentine Gallo becomes a made man, and it's also the day he learns the secrets behind the organization he has served since he was old enough to walk. But it is the mysterious hit woman Jagger Rose that will forever turn his life upside down. Be there when shocking secrets of this new world spill out onto the very first page."-- Provided by publisher.
Identifiers: LCCN 2022026710 (print) | LCCN 2022026711 (ebook) | ISBN 9781506730271 (trade paperback) | ISBN 9781506730431 (ebook)
Subjects: LCGFT: Detective and mystery comics. | Alternative histories (Comics) | Graphic novels.
Classification: LCC PN6728.M866 B46 2023 (print) | LCC PN6728.M866 (ebook) | DDC 741.5/973--dc23/eng/20220708
LC record available at https://lccn.loc.gov/2022026710
LC ebook record available at https://lccn.loc.gov/2022026711

IN MY DAY, THIS CEREMONY WENT A LITTLE DIFFERENTLY.

IT WAS DONE IN A BACKROOM. AWAY FROM THE WORLD.

AND YOU HAD TO EARN IT WITH A LIFETIME OF SERVICE.

YOU HAD TO BE MORE THAN JUST BLOOD.

YOU HAD TO PROVE YOUR WORTH AND LOYALTY.

BUT YOUR FATHER, AND HIS FATHER BEFORE HIM... THEY WERE TRULY HONORABLE MEN.

IN MANY WAYS THEY WERE THE BACKBONE OF THIS ORGANIZATION, THIS FAMILY...

I WOULD MAKE AN EXCEPTION FOR YOU, VALENTINE, EVEN IF OUR WAYS HAD NEVER CHANGED.

TAKE THE KNIFE.

WHO WE ARE IS WHO YOU ARE.

DO YOU AGREE?

YES, SIR.

SHOW US.

THE SENATOR IS IN THERE.

IT'S ONE OF THOSE FANCY BOYS-ONLY, MEMBERS-ONLY CIRCLE JERKS FOR THE ELITE AND POWERFUL.

DON'T GET ANY ON YOU.

LET'S GO.

IT'S ON YOU.

THERE ARE PLACES OUT HERE IN THE WILD WHERE YOU WANT TO WEAR THAT PIN.

THIS IS ONE OF THEM.

ALL RIGHT, JAGGER, LET THE MAN DO HIS THING.

DINO...

YES, PLEASE, DO YOUR *THING*.

MAY I HELP YOU?

I HAVE A PACKAGE FOR SENATOR FULLER.

MAYBE YOU SHOULD GO HOME- SLEEP IT OFF.

SLEEP IT OFF?

DON'T WORRY ABOUT YOUR BOY.

WE'LL TAKE CARE OF THE ARRANGEMENTS.

HELLO? MA.

MA, I'M OK.

WHAT? NO.

NO REASON.

NO. I'M OK.

RIGHT NOW?

MAYBE NOW AIN'T A GOOD TIME, MA.

NO, I'M JUST TIRED- YEAH, I CAN BE THERE IN 20 MINUTES.

YEAH, YEAH, OK...

BAM

BAM

BROOKLYN TODAY

DO YOU KNOW WHAT THE FAMILIES DID TO TAKE CONTROL OF THIS PART OF THE COUNTRY?

DOES HE KNOW WHO HIS GREAT-GRANDFATHER WAS?

NO, HE DON'T.

MA?

JUST LISTEN, VALENTINE.

THE FUCK *IS* THIS?

TAKE A MOMENT. TAKE IT IN.

WHAT AM I SUPPOSED TO SAY HERE? *YOU'RE A RAT?*

JUST LISTEN.

THIS IS WHEN YOU LISTEN.

NO!! I DON'T WANT TO *HEAR ANY MORE!!*

HEY, I DON'T KNOW WHO THE FUCK YOU ARE, FBI GUY!!

YOU'RE LUCKY I DON'T—

IT'S UNDERSTANDABLE TO BE UPSET. WE KNEW THIS WAS GOING TO—

WE'RE ON YOUR SIDE, VALENTINE.

MY SIDE?

MA?

SIT DOWN.

YOU TELL ME EVERYTHING YOU'VE EVER TOLD ME UP UNTIL *THIS MOMENT* HAS BEEN A FUCKING BIG PILE OF SHIT, AND I'M SUPPOSED TO JUST BELIEVE WHAT YOU'RE SAYING NOW?

"WE WERE BOTH BORN INTO THIS. BOTH OF US."

"THE FUCK ARE YOU *TALKING* ABOUT??!! I'M A *MADE GUY* NOW!!"

"WHO CARES ABOUT THAT SHIT?"

"SHAME ON YOU, MA."

STRIP.

COME ON...

CAVITY SEARCH. YOU GOT ANYTHING UP YOUR ASSES?

"OR I HAVE THEM DO IT FOR YOU."

"HANDS OVER YOUR HEADS AND SPIN AROUND."

"NOT EVEN ON MY BIRTHDAY."

"JESUS."

"GOD FUCKING DAMN IT."

"THEY'RE CLEAN."

"THEY'RE CLEAN."

"BE COOL. HERE HE COMES."

"YOUR DRIVER JUST ANALLY RAPED ME."

"THAT'S ON THE HOUSE."

"SOMEONE IS A MOMMA'S BOY."

"I WOULD BE IF I PICKED UP."

"GOOD POINT."

"SHE HEARD ABOUT WHAT HAPPENED IN WASHINGTON."

"SHE'S WORRIED ABOUT ME."

"MUST BE NICE."

"I THINK WE NEED A DO-OVER."

"I'M JAGGER ROSE."

"I'M A HIT PERSON FOR THE FAMILY."

VALENTINE GALLO.

LIFE PARTNERED US UP.

YEAH, HOW 'BOUT THAT?

WHERE DO WE EVEN START?

I KNOW SOME PEOPLE IN THE LUCHIA FAMILY.

MY COUSIN'S GUY IS IN THE GEONEZE.

YOU HAVE A PIECE?

COURSE.

NEVER DON'T HAVE IT ON YOU.

I DON'T LOVE GUNS.

WHAT DO YOU LOVE?

GAMBLING.

WELL, IF YOU DON'T CARRY A PIECE FROM HERE ON OUT YOU'RE GAMBLING ALL RIGHT.

AND ONE MORE THING...

I'M SORRY YOUR FRIEND DIED.

YEAH.

BUT IF I FIND OUT IT WAS YOU WHO BLEW UP THAT SHITHEAD SENATOR...

YOU KNOW I DIDN'T.

FOR THE FIRST TIME IN A LONG TIME I'M NOT SURE WHAT I—

IS THAT PHONE OF YOURS BROKEN?

LEAVE.
LEAVE THE TERRITORY.
LEAVE HERE AND NEVER COME BACK.
HAVE YOUR NEW FRIENDS CHANGE YOUR NAME.
NEVER CALL ME AGAIN.

NEVER.

GGKK!!

SLAMMM

HURRAAGH!!

CRACCKK

BAM BAM BAM

THE BATTLE FOR CLEVELAND 1967

TODAY
THE BROOKLYN PENTHOUSE APARTMENT OF JAGGER ROSE
HIT WOMAN FOR THE BONAVESE FAMILY

WHICH FAMILY?

WHAT?

WHICH FAMILY ARE YOU IDIOTS FROM?

GOODBYE, MISS—

BAM

BAM

SMACK

BITCH!!

NYYAAGGH!

THE FUCK?!

THACK

CRACK

SHIT.
NO FINGERPRINTS.

AND YOU CAME ALONE?
THAT'S INSULTING.

VALENTINE.

SQUEAK

LUCIANO:
BOSS DOMINIC JACKSON

GOLANNO:
BOSS MICHAEL SANGIACOMO

DICASTRO:
BOSS DOC CREA AMUSANTO

                    DON JACKSON
                    Oh yes.

          The days where you old fucks got
          together and whacked each other.

                    DON SANGIACOMO
          We'd get together and build what
            you are sitting on, you piece
                     of shit.

                      DON CREA
          This is a closed-circuit system.
          No one can see or hear us but us.

                    DON SANGIACOMO
                      Says you.

                    DON BONAVESE
                 I am hoping to
             quickly clear the air among
          us and if any of you know why
            and how this happened...

                    DON GIGANTE
          You think it was one of us??!!

                    DON BONAVESE
            It wasn't me or my people
               but it was someone.

                    DON SANGIACOMO
          Maybe the guy you sent fucked it in
          a top hat. Heard it was a kid.

                    DON BONAVESE
          I promise you... I'm looking at
                it from all angles.

                    DON JACKSON
          Wasn't my guys. I can tell you that.

                    DON GIGANTE
          I don't send my guys out of my
          territory and this is exactly fucking
                        why.

                    DON AMUSANTO
          You're going to have Feds up your
          ass, Bonavese. You gave them an excuse.

                    DON SANGIACOMO
          They're going to be up all our
          asses and it's on you as far as
                   I'm concerned.

                    DON BONAVESE
          I was hoping to keep this civil.

                    DON SANGIACOMO
          And I was hoping you wouldn't put us
             in this fucking position.

                    DON JACKSON
          Yo, man, it wasn't him that did
          this. He said it wasn't him- it
          wasn't him. We have to take each
             other on each other's word.

                    DON SANGIACOMO
          If he'd leave our ways well the
          fuck alone and stay to his part
          of the beach, he wouldn't have
          no reason to be sending his
          guys to Washington in the first
          fucking place. This is how we
                  lost Cleveland.

                      DON CREA
             Again, with fucking Cleveland.

                    DON SANGIACOMO
          Yes. Yes, again with fucking Cleveland.

          Those who don't know their history
                 and all that shit...

             Do you know the amount
          of money we left on the table
          when we gave up Cleveland??!!

                    DON JACKSON
        It's Cleveland... so, I'm guessing over two
                    hundred dollars.

                    DON GIGANTE
        Don Bonavese wants to hear it from us and I
        want him to hear it from me... it wasn't us.

                    DON BONAVESE
                Thank you, Don Gigante.

                    DON SANGIACOMO
        Of course, if any of you fucked a donkey
        this bad, the fuck you'd tell any of us.

                    DON GIGANTE
                        True.

                    DON SANGIACOMO
        And if you fucked it on purpose then-

                    DON GIGANTE
            You'd be able to tell. I have a terrible
                        poker face.

                    DON JACKSON
        Anyone else think Sangiacomo is being extra
        fucking rude today? Why don't you calm your
                old ass down and keep it civil.

                    DON SANGIACOMO
        Fuck me then. I guess I'm- I'm old school.
        That means you don't whack United States
        senators and you don't talk about whacking
        United States senators on a fucking TV. You
        want to talk to me? You come fucking see me.

                    DON JACKSON
        Yeah, let's all fly out to Vegas and listen
            to father time rip us a new one.

                    DON AMUSANTO
        You're taking care of this, I assume, Don
                        Bonavese?

                    DON BONAVESE
            Of course. I just want to keep everything
                    aboveboard among us.

                    DON JACKSON
            You'll keep us posted on all this...

                    DON BONAVESE
            And if any of you hear anything...

                    DON GIGANTE
        You know, the old man was right about one
                        thing...

                    DON BONAVESE
                What's that, Carmine?

THIS IS HOW WE LOST CLEVELAND.

MADONNA GALLO... YOU'RE UNDER ARREST.

NEW YORK, 1971

AND SO I TOLD THESE GUYS, YOU SELL NOW YOU'LL BE LOOKING AT NOTHING BUT YOUR DICK IN YOUR—

UH, WARREN, I THINK YOUR NEXT APPOINTMENT IS HERE.

WORLD TRADE CENTER, TODAY

PISSSHHH
PISSSHHH

IS THERE ANY WAY WE GET OUT FROM UNDER THIS?

HISTORY WOULD SAY NO.

BUT I'M SORRY ABOUT YOUR FRIEND.

AND THAT'S THE TRUTH.

MADONNA GALLO.

WHERE AM I?

YOU'RE FBI?

I AM.

I AM GOING TO EXPLAIN WHERE I'M COMING FROM...

YOU SEE, YEARS AGO WHEN YOU CAME TO THE FBI AND YOU TOLD THEM OF YOUR PLAN AND YOUR MOTIVATIONS FOR RAISING YOUR CHILD AS A COVERT DOUBLE AGENT INSIDE THE FAMILY FOR US...

I DON'T THINK YOU'LL FIND IT A SURPRISE TO LEARN THAT THERE WERE SKEPTICS AMONG US, AMONG MY COLLEAGUES...

AMONG THE GENERATION OF AGENTS BEFORE US.

MY NAME IS HACKMAN.

WE'VE NEVER MET BUT I'VE BEEN WORKING ALONGSIDE YOUR CASE FOR A LONG TIME.

WHEN I INHERITED YOUR CASE, I WAS NOT ONE OF THEM.

AND HERE'S WHY...

"YOU SEE WE HAVE SOME THINGS IN COMMON, YOU AND I.

YOU GREW UP UNDER THE GENERATIONAL UMBRELLA OF THE BONAVESE FAMILY.

I GREW UP IN A HOUSEHOLD OF LAW ENFORCEMENT.

I AM FIFTH-GENERATION LAW ENFORCEMENT.

LIKE YOU, I WAS TOLD OF A TIME WHEN THINGS WERE DIFFERENT.

WHERE THERE WAS LAW AND ORDER ACROSS THE ENTIRE NATION.

TIMES BEFORE THIS GOVERNMENT BUCKLED TO THE POWER OF THE FIVE FAMILIES.

I KNOW THAT THE WAY THINGS ARE...IS NOT THE WAY THINGS SHOULD BE.

BUT YOU AND I, WE ARE IN THE MINORITY.

PEOPLE— MOST PEOPLE— JUST WANT THE WAY THINGS ARE TO BE THE WAY THINGS ARE.

MOST PEOPLE JUST WANT TO BE LEFT ALONE WITH THEIR THINGS.

MOST PEOPLE IN THIS WORLD ARE HAPPY THAT THE EAST COAST AND CHICAGO AND VEGAS ARE PLACES WHERE YOU CAN GO AND DO JUST ABOUT ANYTHING TO ANYONE AS LONG AS YOU'RE WILLING TO PAY FOR IT.

HALF THIS COUNTRY IS AN AMUSEMENT PARK FOR FREAKS.

SO I BELIEVE IN THE IDEA THAT THE ONLY WAY TO STOP THIS IS FOR SOMEONE TO BE ON THE INSIDE.

AND THE ONLY WAY TO MAKE THAT HAPPEN IS FOR THEM TO BE BORN AND RAISED.

AND YOU OFFERED UP YOUR SON.

I BELIEVED IN THE IDEA.

BUT YOU FUCKING BLEW IT.

WHAT ARE YOU GOING TO DO TO ME?"

PIER C PARK THE BONAVESE FAMILY HEADQUARTERS

"I DON'T FUCKING UNDERSTAND THIS!!"

"CALM DOWN, PADRINO!"

"CALM DOWN??!! FUCK YOU, CALM DOWN!!"

"DON BONAVESE. A UNITED STATES SENATOR HAS BEEN WHACKED AND IT WAS OUR GUYS THAT WERE THERE. YOU HAVE TO CONSIDER THIS FROM EVERYONE ELSE'S POINT OF VIEW."

"TONY, I KNOW. I GET IT. I UNDERSTAND IT. I KNOW EVERYTHING THAT HAPPENED, I DON'T NEED YOU TO FUCKING REPEAT IT TO ME LIKE I'M SOME FUCKING—"

"BUT YOU DON'T KNOW WHAT'S GOING TO HAPPEN. EVERYTHING— WE HAD THIS, LET'S SAY, BALANCE FOR YEARS. AND WE ALL KNEW THAT THE BALANCE WAS WELL EARNED BUT THAT THE SLIGHTEST THING COULD TIP IT OVER— WE KNEW THIS."

"BUT HERE'S THE THING: THIS AIN'T NO MINOR INFRACTION. A HEAD OF STATE HAS BEEN MURDERED. IT IS AN ACT OF WAR. I TOLD YOU THIS TEN MINUTES AFTER IT HAPPENED: WE ARE AT WAR. ALL OF US. YOU. ARE. AT. WAR."

"THEY WENT TO GO SHOVE THIS RIGHT BACK UP THE GOLANNO FAMILY'S ASS."

TROPICANA HOTEL, LAS VEGAS
TODAY

OK, YOU'RE CUTE. I'LL GIVE IT ONE MORE TRY... YOU FROM OUT OF TOWN?

UH... UH?

YES, ACTUALLY.

YOU HERE ALONE?

UM—

NO, YOU STAY. HE'S ABOUT TO CHANGE THE SIGNAL.

WATCH.

ZAAATTTTT

GYAAGGH!!

TODAY'S YOUR LUCKY DAY.

EVERY TEAM WE CATCH COUNTING, WE TRY, IF WE CAN, TO HAVE A MESSENGER.

THIS GAME...

THIS IS REAL LIFE.

YOU DON'T GET TO COME BACK TO LIFE.

QUEENS 10 YEARS AGO

OW.

SHUT UP.

WOW.

I SWEAR I WAS JUST GOING TO SAY THAT.

"GO FUCK YOURSELF."

"NO BACKUP PLAN?"

"THE PLAN WAS YOU TAKE A SIP OF THE DRINK..."

"OH, THAT'S RIGHT. SO THIS IS THE BACK-UP PLAN. YOUR BACK-UP PLAN NEEDS A BACKUP PLAN."

"BECAUSE, AND PAY ATTENTION HERE, IT MAY BE THAT I AM IN THE SHITHOUSE WITH THE FAMILIES, BUT IF YOU ASSHOLES ARE CAUGHT IN HERE?

IF YOU SO MUCH AS FORGET TO PUT A *COASTER* DOWN? IF YOU'RE CAUGHT IN *OUR* WORLD?

WHAT I DID TO YOUR "FRIENDS" BACK IN BROOKLYN... THAT WAS *NOTHING*.

ANSWER ME THIS..."

"YOU DID."

"WE REALLY DIDN'T. AND I THINK YOU KNOW THAT... FORENSICS AND ALL."

"SO SMUG... YOU'RE TOTALLY GOING TO DIE TODAY."

"OK, SO, LAST WISH."

"WHO KILLED HIM?"

"OK... WE DID. NOT ME, BUT WE. MY PEOPLE."

"WHY?"

"DON BONAVESE... I HAVE TRIED EVERYTHING ELSE.

I AM COMING TO YOU AS AN ABSOLUTE LAST RESORT.

I AM COMING TO YOU... HAT IN HAND.

I AM COMING TO YOU BECAUSE I DON'T KNOW WHAT ELSE TO DO.

ARE YOU FUCKING KIDDING ME WITH THIS??!

THIS INTEL HAS BEEN SHOWN AS HIGH UP THE LADDER AS INTEL GETS SHOWN AND NO ONE IS DOING ANYTHING ABOUT IT.

WHAT ARE— WHAT ARE THEY WAITING FOR?

IT IS MY IMPRESSION THAT THERE ARE FINANCIAL INTERESTS IN THAT REGION THAT ARE KEEPING THEM FROM ACTING...

OIL.

YOU IDIOTS AND YOUR OIL.

WE SHOULD HAVE HAD ELECTRIC CARS TEN YEARS AGO.

YES...

LET'S TALK ABOUT THAT OVER COFFEE ONE DAY.

MEANWHILE...

I'M TRYING TO FIGURE OUT YOUR ANGLE HERE, AGENT STEELBERG.

NEW JERSEY AIRFIELD, ONE WEEK LATER

PENTHOUSE

I CAN'T BELIEVE THIS.

WHAT ABOUT HONOR AND- AND RESPECT AND FAMILY?

WHAT ABOUT THOSE THINGS??

YOU WANT US TO DO IT HERE, PADRINO?

YOU HAVE ANY IDEA WHAT THIS CARPETING COSTS?

NO. TAKE MR. GALLO HERE OUT TO THE DESERT.

RESPECT THE OLD WAYS.

I CAN'T BELIEVE THIS.

PADRINO, CAN I SPEAK WITH YOU FIRST?

CARMELA, JUST SAY WHAT'S ON YOUR MIND.

I'M TRYING TO RESPECT THE OLD WAYS.

AND NOT SAY ANYTHING DISRESPECTFUL IN FRONT OF THE HELP.

I KNOW YOU HAVE A HISTORY WITH THIS JAMOKE.

SO LISTEN TO ME WHEN I TELL YOU THIS...

THIS IS NOT A DRILL!!

SUBBASEMENT 3

YOU FUCKED UP, SPOOK.

YOU FUCKED UP GOOD.

I WAS ALL READY TO POP THESE LITTLE BROOKLYN SHITS.

I WAS THIS CLOSE. ALL READY...

BUT YOU WENT AND WALTZED INTO MY CASINO.

YOU COULDN'T LET THINGS HAPPEN.

NOW I WANT YOU TO ANSWER MISS ROSE'S UNANSWERED QUESTION FROM BEFORE...

WHY? WHY DID THE GOVERNMENT KILL THEIR OWN SENATOR AND TRY TO BLAME IT ON THESE NICE TWO YOUNG TALENTS YOU ALMOST HAD ME KILL?

YOU DO UNDERSTAND THAT I HAVE CAMERAS AND ALL KINDS OF HIGH-TECH SURVEILLANCE-CAMERA SYSTEMS ALL OVER MY HOTEL.

ALL OVER MY CITY.

WE HAVE YOUR CONFESSION.

IT COULD HAVE GONE WORSE, VALENTINE...

YEAH? NO ONE SHOT YOU.

LOT OF GUNS TO MY HEAD TODAY, THOUGH.

COME ON.

YOU STOOD UP FOR ME, CARMELA.

I DID.

IT WAS ALMOST WORTH IT. ALL THIS SHIT—

THAT'S NOT TRUE.

I SAID ALMOST.

HE'S WAITING FOR YOU.

WHICH IS NOT A THING YOU WANT HIM TO DO.

"SPECIAL CIRCUMSTANCES CALL FOR SPECIAL CIRCUMSTANCES.

YOU- AND I DON'T BLAME YOU, BONAVESE- YOU CUT THESE TWO OFF TO SAVE YOUR FAMILY.

BUT THIS VALENTINE GALLO AND JAGGER ROSE ARE INNOCENT.

AND BY DOING SO THE ENEMY REVEALED ITSELF AND CONFESSED.

NOW, YOU WILL ACCEPT THEM BACK INTO YOUR FAMILY, FOR YOU WOULD BE LUCKY TO HAVE THEM...

OR I WILL TAKE THEM GLADLY INTO MINE.

AND NOT ONCE DURING THIS ENTIRE ORDEAL DID THEY DO ANYTHING TO BETRAY THE FAMILIES.

IN FACT, THEY CAME HERE TO BROKER PEACE.

I HAVE AN EMPTY CASINO FOR THE FIRST TIME SINCE IT WAS INVENTED TO PROVE IT.

IF NOT FOR THEM, THIS FUCKED PLAN TO FUCK US MIGHT HAVE WORKED.

THIS- THIS ISN'T THE END OF THIS.

NO SHIT! WE'RE AT FUCKING WAR!!

DO THEY KNOW THAT?

"OF- OF COURSE I WANT THEM BACK.
I WILL SEND FOR THEM.
I WILL MAKE THIS RIGHT.
IT- IT WILL BE MY HONOR."

"DAMN RIGHT. LET ME TELL YOU.
THIS JAGGER ROSE IS PROBABLY THE BEST SOLDIER YOU HAVE.
THIS IS SOMETHING SPECIAL. THESE TWO."

"WE FUCKING TELL THEM.
WE SEND A MESSAGE."

VALENTINE...

MA.

I-

NTERM

SSION

**TO BE CONTINUED...
IN BOOK 2:
UNITED STATES
VS. MURDER INC.**

COVER GALLERY

#1

#2

#3

#4

#5

#6

#1 DAVID MARQUEZ VARIANT

#1 BRIAN MICHAEL BENDIS VARIANT

#2 BRIAN MICHAEL BENDIS VARIANT

#3 BRIAN MICHAEL BENDIS VARIANT

BENDIS!

#4 RAY FAWKES VARIANT

#5 MATT KINDT VARIANT

#1 DAVID MACK VARIANT

#2 DAVID MACK VARIANT

#3 DAVID MACK VARIANT

#4 DAVID MACK VARIANT

#5 DAVID MACK VARIANT

MACK

#6 DAVID MACK VARIANT

MACK

THE UNITED STATES OF MURDER INC.

ISSUE #1 SCRIPT AND SKETCHES
by Brian Michael Bendis and Michael Avon Oeming

PAGE 1

1—Int. Party room/backstage—night

Our hero, Valentine, is looking right at us with a quizzical look as a woman off-panel adjusts the tie on his very nice suit.

VALENTINE
Mom.

2—Over Valentine's shoulder, we see his mother, Madonna, almost tearing up, with glassy eyes. Not tears but very emotional eyes.

She has these huge eyes and these killer dimples. A woman who still keeps herself together. You can tell that back in the day she was quite something.

You can also tell from her big eyes that she has seen a lot of pain and death. A lot of things that have changed her. A lot of secrets that she keeps inside.

Even from her son. Her son being the thing in her life she is most proud of.

MADONNA
Shut up.

VALENTINE
Are you gonna cry?

MADONNA
You want a slap?

3—She adjusts the lapel on his suit. She is so proud of him. All dimples. She holds it together. He looks down at her and can't help but be amazed. Truly.

Behind them, a few silhouettes. Men of means waiting in the wings.

VALENTINE
I've never seen you even come close, Ma.
I'm allowed to declare this an historic event.

MADONNA
Shut your fuckin' mouth.

4—Valentine feels her unconditional love. She knows it's time to let go. The wheels are in motion and there's nothing she can do to stop what's about to happen.

MADONNA (CONT'D)
'M not gonna kiss you because I don't want to get any makeup or nothin' on ya.

VALENTINE

    Go sit, Ma.

    You're freakin' me out.

5—Valentine watches as his mother walks away into the shadows.

OLD MAN (OFF PANEL)

    You ready, Mr. Gallo?

6—Valentine is peeking behind the curtain to the stage. Nothing too obvious, just a slab of light giving him a look at his future.

Behind Valentine, a rotund old man, Bonavese, with a walking cane. Standing behind him ominously. Think Bob Hoskins.

BONAVESE

    Valentine, you ready?

VALENTINE

    Am I, Padrino?

BONAVESE

    Follow me.

PAGE 2

1—Large panel. Over Valentine's shoulder, many men armed with guns, in light suits, are standing around a table. In the center of the table there is a human skull sitting on top of a piece of paper and a knife.

The shadows are so thick behind this ceremony that we can't tell where we are or who else is in the room.

2—Low looking up. Valentine approaches and looks down at . . .

3—Valentine's p.o.v. The human skull sitting on top of a piece of paper and a very ornate knife.

On the piece of paper is the image of a saint.

4—Bonavese picks up the knife and looks at it.

BONAVESE (CONT'D)
> In my day, this ceremony went a little differently.
>
> It was done in a backroom. Away from the world.
>
> And you had to earn it with a lifetime of service.
>
> You had to be more than just blood.
>
> You had to prove your worth and loyalty.

5—Bonavese holds the knife up to Valentine. Showing it to him. Engraved. Old school. Like four-hundred-years-old old school.

BONAVESE (CONT'D)
> But your father, and his father before him . . . they were truly honorable men.
>
> In many ways they were the backbone of this organization, this family . . .
>
> I would make an exception for you, Valentine, even if our ways had never changed.
>
> Take the knife.

6—Valentine holds the knife.

BONAVESE (CONT'D)
> Who we are is who you are.
>
> Do you agree?

VALENTINE
> Yes, sir.

BONAVESE
> Show us.

PAGE 3

1—Valentine holds it to his lower lip. He is getting ready to cut himself.

2—Valentine jabs the knife into the inside of his lower lip.

3—The knife has blood on it.

4—Profile. Valentine leans forward and the blood from the wound drips/pours onto the skull.

BONAVESE (CONT'D)
> You honor your father and your father's father with this blood oath to the family.

5—The blood pours down the front of the skull's face.

6—Bonavese takes the knife himself.

7—Bonavese cuts Valentine's finger.

8—Bonavese takes Valentine's hand and smears Valentine's finger blood on the image of the saint.

PAGES 4–5

Double-page spread

1—From behind Bonavese, Valentine looks to the godfather and wipes his bloody lip. Not sure what is going to happen next.

2—Bonavese picks up the bloody image of the saint. Another man hands him a long match already lit.

3—Bonavese lights the image of the saint on fire.

4—The paper is burning quickly as Bonavese hands it to Valentine.

BONAVESE (CONT'D)
> If you betray your family . . .
>
> Your flesh will burn like this saint.

5—Valentine looks at the burning paper in his hand. The saint is burning.

6—The burning paper is almost gone and about to burn Valentine's fingers.

7—*Valentine winces, as it clearly hurts. A test of endurance.*

8—*Valentine opens his fingers and the piece of burning paper floats into the air. Embers.*

VALENTINE

>Ah!

9—*The piece of burning paper disappears as it burns itself out.*

10—*The piece of paper is gone. Just a tiny swirl of smoke.*

11—*Bonavese pulls out a small gold pin. A circular pin with a symbol on it. A dagger pointed down.*

12—*Bonavese puts the pin on Valentine's lapel.*

13—*Valentine turns to see the boss smiling. The serious part is over.*

BONAVESE

>And that's that.

14—*All the men are smiling and parting ways . . . some shaking his bloody hand. Bonavese claps his hands and yells out.*

BONAVESE (CONT'D)

>Let's eat!!

15—*Valentine takes all the goodwill from his fellow soldiers. His lip still bleeding. A spotlight on him as he looks out and sees . . .*

PAGES 6–7

Double-page spread

Wide of the party room.

We now see the entire Bonavese family is there. Hundreds of tables of people of all shapes and sizes. Dozens of good families. Mothers, fathers, wives, husbands, children, and grandmothers and grandfathers . . . cousins.

In the old days, the days before things went differently, this ceremony was done in secret in a secret backroom, but now that the families are an established part of society, this ceremony is done in public, in front of the people, like a bar mitzvah or a wedding.

The ceremony part is over and the catering is about to begin. There will be eating and drinking and dancing.

This was Valentine's ceremony. He is a made man.

2—*On the bottom of the spread we see that table number one features his mother, Madonna, clapping, still with glassy eyes but no tears.*

Other members of his family that really won't play any part of this story.

Except for another guy his same age. His cousin Dino. Thick, strong, curly haired, multicultural. We imagine his dad was a made guy and his mother was a hooker who had Dino out of wedlock to the embarrassment of many. Good guy, good friend, but he is a point of gossip and pity.

Dino is so happy. Applauding. Yelling. This is the best day of their lives.

DINO

>Oh my god!!
>
>Fuck yeah!!

MADONNA

>Be quiet, Dino.

DINO

>This is CRAZY!!
>
>He did so good!!

PAGE 8

1—Ext. Hoboken, New Jersey

2—Ext. Street

3—Ext. Pier C park

The Bonavese family headquarters is actually built on the Pier C park structure. Instead of being a park it is a family business compound.

Instead of the compound being hidden away, it is what anyone would see as the real estate crown jewel of New Jersey.

This subtle difference shows the family business is done out in the open in opulence. It says everything about what's different about our world.

This isn't a sci-fi flying-car alternate reality. This is basically our reality with the subtle differences that the mob is doing things out in the open—everything from timeless rituals to how and where they live.

A stunning mansion is built on this pier. A small fleet of yachts.

4—From behind a man's hand holding a tomato drink that may or may not have alcohol in it . . . Valentine is walking across the pier to the opening of the guarded gate.

It is not guarded like a mob compound but like the way the White House is guarded.

Valentine looks good.

5—From behind Valentine, Myer Bloom, a handsome Jewish mob lawyer, is enjoying his drink and coming up to shake Valentine's hand.

MYER BLOOM

>Mr. Gallo.

VALENTINE

>Mr. Bloom.

MYER BLOOM

>First time at the pier?

VALENTINE

>Yes, sir.

MYER BLOOM

>Hell of a party last night.

VALENTINE

>Thank you for that.
>
>Really.

6—They shake hands. All this is new to Valentine. This is his first meeting this high up the food chain.

He doesn't know what to expect and everyone's friendly faces and politeness are blowing his mind.

MYER BLOOM

Don't thank me.

I just do what the big guy says.

How did the rest of your night go?

PAGE 9

1—Int. Hotel room—night

Flashback! Valentine is riding the hell out of a busty hooker while another is behind him. We imagine she is shoving her pinkie, or something else, right up his ass.

The room is trashed. A champagne bottle is open on the bed and soaking the sheet as the three ride each other feverishly.

He is shocked at the experience. This is not every day.

2—Ext. Pier C park

Resume! Valentine and Myer are walking toward us.

VALENTINE

    All right.

MYER BLOOM

    You can thank him for that too.

    He's waiting for you.

3—Valentine is escorted through a lovely, well-kept garden. Bonavese is in a cobblestone garden. A couple of garden-style fancy tables and chairs. The place is perfect.

Bonavese is being served tea by a gorgeous Korean woman.

Another sharp-dressed but relaxed older man, fit, is greeting Valentine. His name is Tony Tuzzo. The underboss.

TONY TUZZO

    Valentine.

VALENTINE

    Mr. Tuzzo.

4—Valentine sits at a small table with Tony. Mr. Bonavese is sipping his tea at another table with a tablet and a newspaper and his tea.

TONY TUZZO

    So, you ready to get down to it?

VALENTINE

    Course.

TONY TUZZO

    You understand you won't be working the poker games in town anymore.

VALENTINE

    I actually DIDN'T know that.

TONY TUZZO

    You're a made guy now.

    You don't need to be wipin' college shitheads' asses anymore.

    You're eventually gonna have people doin' that for you.

VALENTINE

So, uh, what WILL I be doing?

5—Tony looks over to Bonavese, Bonavese doesn't even look at them.

BONAVESE

Tell him.

6—Over Valentine's shoulder. Tony pulls out a square metal suitcase, small and oddly shaped, and puts it on the table.

TONY TUZZO

Today you're going on a little trip. As a representative of OURS.

VALENTINE

Oh.

TONY TUZZO

You're gonna go to DC and deliver this to a guy.

7—Valentine is shocked because . . .

VALENTINE

DC?

Washington, DC?

PAGE 10

1—Tony is laughing at his stupid question. Bonavese isn't even looking at them. He seems to be reading his paper.

TONY TUZZO

Is there another DC? This guy!

VALENTINE

Oh, I've, uh, I've never left the territories before.

TONY TUZZO

Yeah, I imagine.

Why the fuck would ya? Nothin' out there.

VALENTINE

So, I, uh . . .

>   What do I do exactly?

2—*Tony hands him a cash envelope clearly full of cash.*

> **TONY TUZZO**
>
>   You'll take the train down ta DC, you'll stay at the Ambassador for the night, deliver this to our guy, and you'll come home tomorrow.
>
> **VALENTINE**
>
>   I'm leaving tonight?
>
> **TONY TUZZO**
>
>   Yeah.
>
> **VALENTINE**
>
>   You don't want me to drive?
>
>   I can drive.

3—*Tony is clearly saying that this is the last time you question an order. Handing him a cash envelope.*

> **TONY TUZZO**
>
>   You'll take the train down ta DC, you'll stay at the Ambassador for the night, deliver this to our guy, and you'll come home tomorrow.
>
> **VALENTINE**
>
>   OK.
>
> **TONY TUZZO**
>
>   This is your—let's call it a per diem.

4—*Valentine knows not to count the cash in front of them even though he is clearly dying to.*

> **VALENTINE**
>
>   Who am I meeting?

5—*Tony has a small tablet. Showing him a picture of an African American senator.*

> **TONY TUZZO**
>
>   Senator Idis Fuller.
>
> **VALENTINE**
>
>   A senator?
>
>   Is he expecting me?

6—Tony gives him a look that says this is more dangerous than you think.

TONY TUZZO

No.

But the asshole SHOULD be.

He'll have a lot of questions.

But he'll open the case and then he won't have any more questions.

HE opens it, not you.

7—Valentine is stunned by all of this but tries to keep it cool. Not sure if he should ask but . . .

VALENTINE

Do, I, uh, get a receipt?

PAGE 11

1—Over Valentine's shoulder. Tony belly laughs.

TONY TUZZO

What the fuck are you talking about?

2—Valentine does not like being laughed at or talked down to. He feels embarrassed in front of the godfather.

VALENTINE

Am I—I don't think these questions are stupid.

I've never done nothin' like this before.

I should walk out of here not knowin' what the fuck I'm doing?

3—Tony rolls his eyes and calms himself. He sees the kid is pissed even though he doesn't care. No disrespect was meant.

TONY TUZZO

Nah-uh. No.

You don't get a receipt.

You come back here, you say: package delivered.

4—Over Tony's shoulder. Valentine is looking over to the godfather. Not sure if he's taking this too far.

VALENTINE

Can I bring someone?

TONY TUZZO

No.

VALENTINE

I've—I've never left the territories before. I'd like to bring someone.

5—Over Valentine's shoulder. Bonavese finally looks at him. Did Valentine just insult him even though he didn't mean to? Bonavese doesn't take his eyes off the newspaper.

BONAVESE

Your shmuck of a cousin?

VALENTINE

He's not a—with all due respect.

BONAVESE

His father was a whoremongering shmuck and HE is a shmuck.

6—Over Tony's shoulders, Valentine on the left, and the godfather on the right, Valentine isn't sure if he should keep this going but . . .

VALENTINE

I can vouch for him.

TONY TUZZO

Jesus!

BONAVESE

No you can't.

But you're one of us. It's your call.

And it's on YOUR tab.

I'm not payin' out for that half a whore.

7—Valentine holds the envelope in one hand and touches the case with the other. Basically downloading all of this information. Making sure he is clear.

VALENTINE

Yes, sir.

8—Bonavese looks at him for the first time. Completely annoyed.

BONAVESE

Valentine . . .

Go away.

PAGES 12–13

Double-page spread

1—Ext. Bullet train to Washington, DC

Thin panel across both pages.

DINO
Fuck me.

2—Int. Train

First-class cabin.

Valentine and Dino are taking their seats in the first-class cabin. They sit on the opposite end of the cabin from a handful of slimy young Wall Street assholes that are gathered around the first-class open bar.

They are chasing the Asian lady bartender out of the cabin with their obnoxious behavior. They are drunk and coked up and headed to some Georgetown party they think is going to kick ass but probably won't.

One guy in particular looks like a young John Turturro. He is named Eddie.

Valentine has the case and is calm and cool. Dino is looking out the window like a puppy. A little underdressed but so excited.

WALL STREET ASSHOLE
Oh come on, baby, if I wanted that look I'd'a stayed at home.

WALL STREET ASSHOLE 2
Good one.

VALENTINE
Be cool, Dino.

DINO
We're leavin' the territory. This is crazy!

VALENTINE
Are you bein' cool?

2—Two shot. Dino sits in the same couch-like seat as Valentine. Looking at him with love. Valentine feels his look and ignores it.

3—Same.

DINO
You vouched for me.

VALENTINE
I need a human shield.

DINO

>You love me.

4—Dino and Valentine watch the Wall Street assholes trip over themselves to run the Asian bartender out of the cabin.

WALL STREET ASSHOLE

>I mean I want ACTUAL sex on an ACTUAL beach!!

WALL STREET ASSHOLE 2

>Oh!!

VALENTINE

>Look at all these Wall Street shmucks. One day to get away from them and there they are.

DINO

>Hey, fuck 'em.
>
>They pay up just like the rest of us.

VALENTINE

>Assholes.

5—Dino and Valentine watch as Eddie is tripping over himself and spilling his drink. Laughing at whatever he just did or said. Spilling a drink.

DINO

>For real.

VALENTINE

>I know that one guy.

DINO

>Yeah?

VALENTINE

>What's HE leavin' the territory for?

6—Dino and Valentine. Dino looks to the left. Valentine staring at the Wall Streeters on the right.

DINO

>He's allowed to.
>
>Hey, where'd the redhead from the platform go?

VALENTINE

    Back in steerage.

7—Over Dino and Valentine's shoulder. Eddie stands up and drunkenly points at Valentine. Just recognizing him through his drunken haze.

EDDIE

    Hey, I know you.

    You deal the cards down at you-know-where!

VALENTINE

    Go siddown, Eddie.

8—From behind Valentine, Eddie, drunk and stumbling, looks like he is looking for a fight.

EDDIE

    The fuck you say to me??

VALENTINE

    I said go sit down.

    Asshole.

9—Low looking up. Eddie, drunk, about to punch Valentine right in the nose but stops.

10—Eddie's p.o.v. The pin.

11—Same as nine. Eddie stops himself because he knows what the pin means.

12—Valentine looks at him with a cocked eyebrow that says: yeah, go sit the fuck down.

PAGES 14–15

Double-page spread

1—Big panel. Dino is up on his feet and clocks Eddie right in the jaw. Hard. No one fucks with his friend.

SPX: WHACK

2—"Camera" on the floor. Eddie hits the floor. His nose blood sprays. Dino is already kicking him.

SPX: FUMP

EDDIE

    Oh!

3—Eddie's p.o.v. Low looking up and wide. Eddie's Wall Street friends are stunned. Looking down shocked.

4—Same. Eddie's Wall Street friends all point and burst out and laugh at him.

WALL STREET ASSHOLE

    Aaaaahahahahahaha!!

WALL STREET ASSHOLE 2

    Douchebag!!

5—*Dino sits down. Valentine is annoyed but at the same time grateful.*

VALENTINE

He WAS backing off.

DINO

I already had my arm cocked.

I couldn't stop.

VALENTINE

And the kick.

DINO

It's my signature move.

6—*Eddie, shaking, crawls to his drunk asshole friends. They laugh at him and throw dollar bills. They make it rain on him.*

WALL STREET ASSHOLE

Tough guy!!

WALL STREET ASSHOLE (CONT'D)

Come on, honey, give me a lap dance.

WALL STREET ASSHOLE 2

That doesn't even make any sense!

7—*Dino and Valentine. Valentine concedes a thank-you. Dino, looking off panel to the left, is already deciding to go find the redhead.*

VALENTINE

Thank you.

DINO

I'm gonna go find the redhead.

VALENTINE

I said thank you.

8—*From over Valentine's head, Dino leaves the car as a woman enters. In the shadows we can just tell a woman is coming in. Pink and purple hair.*

DINO

Yeah yeah . . .

9—*Valentine cocks an eyebrow as he sees . . .*

PAGE 16

1—Page tall. Enter our female lead. Our femme fatale. JAGGER ROSE. She looks amazing. She enters first class and surveys all that she sees. She oozes sex and violence.

She owns the room by walking in. Nothing slutty, just smoldering. A practiced, perfected move.

2—Valentine watches her as Jagger moves over to the bar and the Wall Street idiots. Eddie plugging his nose with tissues as she steps over him.

His drunk friends are very taken with her. All eyes on her and she knows it.

3—The drunk Wall Streeters watch Jagger slide behind the bar, drop her coat, and start making a mixed drink.

She looks amazing. Nonplussed.

4—Eddie drops on the bar and snarls at her.

EDDIE
A whiskey.

5—Jagger continues making her drink. Ignoring him.

6—Eddie has had enough shit for one day.

EDDIE (CONT'D)
Which part of WHISKEY do you not under—

PAGE 17

1—From behind Eddie. Jagger takes the bottle she's holding and smashes it over his head. Hard.

2—Valentine watches, surprised, as Eddie hits the ground and his friends point in her face to protect him and protest her.

WALL STREET ASSHOLE
You DUMB BITCH!!

WALL STREET ASSHOLE 2
I'm gonna have your JOB, Sally!

3—Jagger pulls a gun on them. Really nonplussed.

JAGGER ROSE
Name's not Sally.

Get off the train.

4—The Wall Street guys are shocked. Some laughing.

WALL STREET ASSHOLE 2
The fuck you say to—

5—Jagger casually SHOOTS HER GUN as she takes a sip of her drink.

SPX: BAM

PAGES 18–19

Double-page spread

1—The Wall Streeters freak the fuck out. She grazed one of their arms but she certainly changed the mood of the conversation.

WALL STREET ASSHOLE

What the FUCK??!

2—Jagger is enjoying her drink. Smoking gun up.

Who's next?

3—From behind Jagger, who pours another drink, gun still up, the Wall Streeters stumble out past Valentine.

Eddie on the floor. Out cold and bleeding.

WALL STREET ASSHOLE

Fucking god damn!

WALL STREET ASSHOLE (CONT'D)

What fucking kind of train?

WALL STREET ASSHOLE (CONT'D)

Let's just GO!!

I'm bleeding!!

Shot me!!

4—Valentine calmly watches as Jagger steps over Eddie's body with the two drinks. Heading toward him.

VALENTINE

How much are they paying YOU to bartend?

I think I can get you something better in the city . . .

JAGGER ROSE

I'm not the bartender, you ass.

5—Jagger offers him a drink and sits in Dino's seat.

Here we get a sense of their chemistry. They are very different from Walker and Deena.

Although she is a fierce opponent and a feisty broad, she is steely eyed and in control, while Deena is wild, nervous energy.

Valentine is young, a few years younger than her, and very into her. He is trying to be cool but years away from being able to pull it off. But still charming.

VALENTINE

Thank you.

Who ARE you?

JAGGER ROSE

    A girl comes onto your train, shows a gun, shoots a guy, and you just sit here?

VALENTINE

    Well, I don't like to judge.

JAGGER ROSE

    No, I'm serious.

    How do you know that I'm not here to take the briefcase from you?

6—He sips his drink. He somehow never considered it but maybe he should have. But he still doesn't think it is an issue.

She is sipping her drink and rolling her eyes.

VALENTINE

    Huh.

    Dunno.

JAGGER ROSE

    Sexist.

VALENTINE

    No.

JAGGER ROSE

    If I was a guy—

VALENTINE

    You'd look terrible in that outfit.

7—She looks at him. Smolder. He puts his foot on the briefcase as to half block it.

JAGGER ROSE

    You know exactly what I mean.

VALENTINE

    You don't know what's in the briefcase.

JAGGER ROSE

    No.

    YOU don't know what's in it.

8—Same. She sips. He thinks to himself.

JAGGER ROSE (CONT'D)

You don't fucking RECOGNIZE me, do you?

VALENTINE

Um . . .

JAGGER ROSE

Really.

VALENTINE

Did we—?

9—Flashback! To the sex party last night. He's trying to think if she was one of the call girls. She wasn't. It might be funny to use a stat of the same panel from previously.

10—Same as 8. He decides she wasn't there but he's not a hundred percent. She rolls her eyes to the sky.

VALENTINE (CONT'D)

No, that wasn't you . . .

JAGGER ROSE

Jesus help me.

11—Same. Valentine holds out his hand to shake. She doesn't accept. Back to sip her drink.

VALENTINE

Hi, I'm—

JAGGER ROSE

Valentine. I KNOW.

I went to school with your sister.

12—Same. He is stunned. She is subtly annoyed.

VALENTINE

We did? You did?

JAGGER ROSE

Yes. I've slept over at your house.

VALENTINE

Shit, I'm sorry.

You're—um—you're—

13—Same. She drinks. Muttering to herself.

JAGGER ROSE
Jagger—Jagger Rose.

God damn it.

VALENTINE
OK.

JAGGER ROSE
Fuck you.

VALENTINE
How many colors was your hair back then?

14—Same.

JAGGER ROSE
Put the pin away.

VALENTINE
What?

JAGGER ROSE
The coronation pin.

Put it away.

15—Angle on his made-man pin on his lapel.

PAGE 20

1—Jagger takes the pin and puts it under his lapel. He still wears it but not so anyone can see. He is a little put off.

JAGGER ROSE (CONT'D)
We're clearing Baltimore, which means that little pin just became an ARREST ME pin.

VALENTINE
Hey.

JAGGER ROSE
You are out of the territory and you are out here without a net.

2—Jagger goes back to her drink. Valentine is genuinely stunned.

VALENTINE
>Who are you?

JAGGER ROSE
>Don Bonavese sent me.

VALENTINE
>HE sent you?
>
>To do what?

3—Jagger looks him over. He is trying not to look at her cleavage.

JAGGER ROSE
>Keep an eye on you.

VALENTINE
>He didn't say anything about you.

JAGGER ROSE
>I know. He finds it funny.

VALENTINE
>You're here to escort me?

4—Jagger sits back and watches him try not to stare at her boobs.

JAGGER ROSE
>I'm not an escort.
>
>I'm here to protect you.

VALENTINE
>What?

JAGGER ROSE
>Deal with it.

VALENTINE
>I got a guy.

JAGGER ROSE
>Yeah? Where is he?

VALENTINE
>Good point.

5—From behind Jagger and Valentine, a couple of guys from train security who look just like us come in and see the crazy mess.

TRAIN SECURITY
>What the—
>
>What the fuck is going on in here?

PAGE 21

1—Jagger pulls out a couple of folded hundreds and smoothly hands them to him.

JAGGER ROSE
>Excuse us.
>
>We're on a date.

2—The security guy takes the cash. His partner eyeballing his half over his shoulder.

TRAIN SECURITY
>Yeah, uh, OK.

JAGGER ROSE
>Thanks.

3—Jagger leans back and takes a drink. No big deal. He stares at her. In awe now more than any leering.

4—Same. She doesn't even look at him.

JAGGER ROSE (CONT'D)
>It'll never happen.

VALENTINE
>What?

JAGGER ROSE
>I will never sleep with you.

5—Same. Valentine is uncomfortable. Jagger is a rock. Enjoying her beverage.

VALENTINE
>Excuse me.

JAGGER ROSE
>Your penis will NEVER be in my vagina.
>
>It'll never happen.

VALENTINE

Yeah, well . . . Never say never.

JAGGER ROSE

It'll NEVER happen.

6—Same. He leans forward. Uncomfortable. Eyeing her out of the side of his eye. Jagger knows it.

7—Same.

JAGGER ROSE (CONT'D)

Touch my boob.

VALENTINE

What?

PAGE 22

1—Valentine sits up and looks at her. She has not budged. Sitting back with her drink.

JAGGER ROSE

Touch my boob.

All guys think about when they see boobs is how much they want to touch them.

We have work to do.

Touch my boob, right now, demystify them, get it out of your system . . . and you can focus.

2—Same.

VALENTINE

No.

JAGGER ROSE

Last chance.

3—Same. Valentine can't believe her. She sips her drink.

4—Same. Valentine thinks about it. He wants to . . .

5—Same. Valentine reaches out and almost touches her boob. She doesn't flinch.

6—Same. Valentine decides against it. She doesn't budge.

VALENTINE

No.

JAGGER ROSE

OK.

Offer rescinded.

We understand each other?

VALENTINE

You're nuts.

JAGGER ROSE

Then we understand each other.

Hey look . . .

PAGE 23

1—Ext. Washington, DC

The train is pulling into the beautiful Washington, DC. Iconic.

But it is not that opulent. The air is terrible. Sickly. As if something has happened where the air is actually cleaner in the territory than it is in the rest of the world.

JAGGER ROSE NARRATION

"We're in THEIR nation's capital."

2—Int. Train station

Dino, Val, and Jagger are walking through the train station. The Wall Street guys are keeping their distance.

Others mill about.

Tons of uniformed angry cops walking around or standing tall. The first cops we have seen.

VALENTINE

Strike out?

DINO

Couldn't find her. Who is SHE?

VALENTINE

Says she went to school with my sister.

DINO

SHE—OH DAMN. She did.

Hey, BRACES.

3—Jagger turns around and looks at him as if to say: Do you think that's really how this is going to go? He holds up his hands in surrender. He meant no disrespect.

DINO (CONT'D)

You—hey, oh OK. You look much better.

JAGGER ROSE

    I know.

    THANK you.

4—From behind Val. Val stops at the newsstand and sees the one that catches his eye.

The book: The United States of Murder Incorporated: How the United States Government Gave Up the East Coast to the Mob. By Shecky Finklestien.

Other books include: Mice Templar—NOW A MAJOR MOTION PICTURE, Takio the YA novel by Olivia, etc.

5—Jagger Rose sees what Valentine is looking at. Dino is staring at one of the cops like he is an alien from outer space.

JAGGER ROSE (CONT'D)

    That's a funny one.

    An oral history and no one is sayin' nothin'.

PAGES 24–25

Double-page spread

1—Ext. Washington, DC/private club—day

A secret club. A members-only club. Something very Skull and Bones. A type of club for very wealthy and powerful people.

2—Ext. Street

Across the street, Jagger, Valentine, and Dino are watching. Dino still underdressed. Already bored.

Behind them a cobblestone half wall and a black spiked fence separating them from a small city park.

JAGGER ROSE (CONT'D)

    The senator is in there.

    It's one of those fancy boys-only, members-only circle jerks for the elite and powerful.

    Don't get any on you.

VALENTINE

    Let's go.

JAGGER ROSE

    It's on you.

3—Valentine looks at Jagger as she gestures to him like a game show hostess. People mill about. The sidewalk is crowded.

JAGGER ROSE (CONT'D)

    The don said this was on you, and that is a boys-only club.

    Put the pin on.

VALENTINE
    You told me to take it off.

4—Jagger puts it back where she originally unpinned it from. Dino doesn't like her.

JAGGER ROSE
    And now I'm telling you to put it on.

    There are places out here in the wild where you want to wear that pin.

    This is one of them.

5—Int. Club

From behind the guard/host at the opulent dark-wood, low-light front desk. Valentine walks into the club with the case. Backlit to the front door light.

DESK MANAGER
    May I help you?

VALENTINE
    I have a package for Senator Fuller.

6—The man at the desk is about to shoo him away but . . .

7—The desk clerk's p.o.v. He sees the pin.

8—The host picks up the phone and at the same time points Valentine down the dark wood hall full of paintings and trophies.

DESK MANAGER
    Down the hall.

    Third room on your right.

    The Dupont Club, may I help you?

9—Doorway—Valentine enters a doorway and looks down at . . .

PAGE 26

1—Over Valentine's shoulder. The senator is a very tall African American. Sixty.

VALENTINE
    Senator Fuller?

2—The senator looks up from his paper with a politician's shit phony smile.

3—Small panel. Angle on the pin.

4—Same as 2. His smile drops. He knows what this is.

SENATOR
    How the fuck did you even get in—never mind.

5—Valentine hands over the case. The senator looks at it.

SENATOR (CONT'D)
    And am I supposed to open this now?

VALENTINE
    That's completely up to you.

SENATOR
    I don't understand you people.

6—Low looking up. Fuller is genuinely pissed.

SENATOR (CONT'D)
    You have everything you said you wanted.

    You have an entire chunk of the country with which to do what you may.

    And STILL it is not enough.

    You're too young to remember what things were like before—this . . .

    THIS is insane.

7—The senator opens up the case and looks inside.

PAGE 27

1—Over the senator's shoulder. It is a foam molded case. Two compartments. On the left, a beautifully stacked large pile of thousand-dollar bills in a perfectly cased foam setting.

Right next to it is a dead, bloody bird. Bloody. Also encased.

2—The senator looks at him with complete contempt.

SENATOR (CONT'D)
    Message received.

    Thank you.

3—Valentine is not sure what he is supposed to do now. Should he leave?

4—The senator wants him to leave.

SENATOR (CONT'D)
    Is there a singing telegram portion of this message?

    No?

    Then goodbye.

5—Ext. Club

Valentine walks out of the club into the sunny, crowded street.

6—Int. Club

The senator is so angry. Looking in the case.

7—Ext. Street

Over Valentine's shoulder. Jagger, across the street eating a hot dog, is about to throw it away when . . .

8—Int. Club

The senator slams down the case in anger.

PAGES 28–29

Double-page spread

Boom. The entire front of the building explodes. The street erupts into chaos.

People and cars get hurt. Fire. Blood.

Valentine goes flying into a metal gate across the street. He really took a hit.

PAGE 30

1—Jagger picks herself up. Head ringing. She is scraped and injured.

2—Jagger dives and puts the fire out on a stunned and struggling Valentine's shoulder.

3—Valentine looks up. Dazed. Head bleeding. Confused.

4—Over Valentine's shoulder. Dino is dead. As are many others.

Dino is impaled on the thick black fence that was separating the sidewalk from the small city park.

5—Valentine, horrified, dirty, sooty, stares at us. He's in shock. He didn't know what to expect from all of this but he certainly didn't expect any of this.

PAGE 31

1—Ext. Funeral home/backroom—night

Dino lies in the closed casket. The casket is in perspective toward us. At the end of it, Valentine is still in shock. His head is bandaged.

Clearly they have gotten themselves and Dino out of Washington and back to New York.

2—Over Valentine's shoulder, on the other side of this long, cluttered funeral home backroom full of coffin parts and wreaths and other things, Jagger is having a heated conversation with Tony and Myer. Clearly something went wrong. Something is wrong. Whatever it is, Jagger was not in on it. That is for sure.

The mobsters look panicked but are keeping it together. Trying to figure out what happened.

> **JAGGER ROSE**
> (muffled)
> Didn't even tell him I was coming and the fucking case was rigged??!!

> **TONY TUZZO**
> (muffled)
> It wasn't!

> **JAGGER ROSE**
> (muffled)
> Are you fucking kidding me??!

3—Valentine squints. Mistrusting. Bloodshot eyes. Unshaven. Did they send him there to die? Did they send him there on a suicide mission without telling him?

4—*Over Valentine's shoulder. Myer has had enough of Jagger's accusatory shit. Tony is walking up to Valentine with purpose.*

MYER BLOOM

(muffled)

Enough!! OK??!! Enough!!

Everyone is fucking upset, god damn it!!

TONY TUZZO

I want to hear it from you.

You talked to the guy? The senator?

5—*Tony is right in Valentine's face. Reading his face. Looking for clues of a lie. Valentine is bubbling with rage.*

VALENTINE

I walked into the club, I handed him the briefcase.

TONY TUZZO

He opened it in front of you?

VALENTINE

Yeah.

TONY TUZZO

You saw what was inside?

VALENTINE

Yeah.

TONY TUZZO

What did he say?

6—*Valentine squints. Bloodshot eyes. Unshaven.*

VALENTINE

He said you were greedy fucking assholes and told me to fuck off.

7—*Valentine's p.o.v. Tony and Myer look at him. Not sure if the insult is coming from him or from the dead senator. Jagger pacing behind them.*

PAGE 32

Ten equal-size panels. All tight. Suspense.

1—*Tony is trying to put this together.*

TONY TUZZO

That's exactly what he said?

BIGGER?

2—*Valentine is exhausted.*

> **VALENTINE**
> I'm paraphrasing, but yeah.

3—*Same as 1.*

> **TONY TUZZO**
> Did he close the case in front of you?

4—*Same as 2.*

> **VALENTINE**
> I don't—I don't know.

5—*Same as 1.*

> **TONY TUZZO**
> It's important.

6—*Valentine has no idea what he is thinking.*

> **VALENTINE**
> Why?

7—*Tony doesn't understand how Valentine doesn't understand . . .*

> **TONY TUZZO**
> Because we're trying to determine if it was the briefcase that did the job.

8—*Valentine is confused.*

> **VALENTINE**
> Of COURSE it was.

9—*Myer leans in . . . trying to get this in his head. Sincere. Sweating.*

> **MYER BLOOM**
> Valentine, listen to me . . .
>
> We wouldn't do that to you.

10—*Valentine doesn't know this to be true.*

> **VALENTINE**
> Why not?

PAGE 33

Ten equal-size panels. All tight. Suspense.

3 PEEPS TALK

BOM.

1—*Same as 9, last page.*

MYER BLOOM

You're one of us.

2—*Valentine is bubbling with rage.*

VALENTINE

My friend is DEAD.

3—*Tony points at us. Totally sincere.*

TONY TUZZO

Hey, that's on YOU!

We told you not to bring him.

4—*Same as 2.*

VALENTINE

You're saying YOU didn't do this.

5—*Tony holds up his hand. Sincere.*

TONY TUZZO

I swear on Christ Almighty.

6—*Same as 4.*

VALENTINE

I want to hear it from him.

I want to hear it from Don Bonavese.

7—*Myer holds up his hands. There's nothing to discuss.*

MYER BLOOM

That can't happen at the moment.

8—*Valentine doesn't trust any of this.*

VALENTINE

Why not?

9—*Same as 7.*

MYER BLOOM

He's not here.

He left for the old country.

10—*Valentine clearly doesn't believe them.*

PAGES 34–35

Double-page spread

1—*On the other side of the room, Jagger is pacing. She is clearly shaken as well. She may be on Val's side more than he thinks.*

Three men in the background.

TONY TUZZO
Maybe you should go home—sleep it off.

VALENTINE
SLEEP IT OFF?

TONY TUZZO
Don't worry about your boy.

We'll take care of the arrangements.

2—*Over Valentine's shoulder. Myer sees Valentine doesn't believe them and understands.*

MYER BLOOM
This is bad business, Val. This is not what we do.

We don't send our soldiers on suicide missions.

We'd HAVE no soldiers.

You see that, right?

3—*Valentine sees the logic but . . . Val's phone rings.*

SPX: GLEE GLEE

4—*Valentine looks at his iPhone. It's his mom. The mobsters argue behind him.*

Reads: Mom

TONY TUZZO
Someone got to the case.

MYER BLOOM
It wasn't THE CASE!!

TONY TUZZO
It wasn't the case?? The case just happens to be—

5—*Valentine puts a finger to his ear and turns away from them and answers.*

VALENTINE
Hello? Ma.

Ma, I'm OK.

What? No.

No reason.

6—Valentine is walking away from the gangsters as he talks to his mom. Finger to his ear. Annoyed.

VALENTINE (CONT'D)

No. I'm OK.

Right now?

Maybe now ain't a good time, Ma.

No, I'm just tired—yeah, I can be there in 20 minutes.

Yeah, yeah, OK . . .

7—Valentine, without breaking his stride, hangs up and keeps walking toward us and away from the mobsters.

VALENTINE (CONT'D)

I gotta go.

TONY TUZZO

Best you not say nothin' to no one till we know what the score is.

MYER BLOOM

We'll get to the bottom of this, Valentine.

We always do.

TONY TUZZO

We always do.

8—Valentine is most of the silhouette foreground. Walking away from them. All we can see past him is Jagger hugging herself.

PAGES 36–37

Double-page spread

1—Ext. Brooklyn street

Valentine, lost in dark thought and despair, walks through the streets of Brooklyn. Colorful and alive. These people feel protected. These people are very used to a very specific way of life.

The families have protected this area for so long that they don't know any other way of life.

2—Valentine comes to the steps of his mother's nice brownstone. She's dressed smart and already at the door atop the small staircase.

MADONNA

What the hell happened to your head?

3—Valentine has climbed the steps. She is looking at his bandage and isn't happy.

VALENTINE

Nothin'.

MADONNA

    My ass.

VALENTINE

    It's nothing.

MADONNA

    A made guy three days and already someone bashed your fucking head in.

VALENTINE

    Ma.

MADONNA

    Get in here.

4—Int. Mom's brownstone

Inside her very average, very well-kept apartment. Not exactly an old-school Italian apartment . . . something more modern.

A classy, smart, modern woman who has had the place to herself for a while. She is doing something nice with it. We imagine that Valentine has made sure that she hasn't ever needed money.

She is walking him toward us.

VALENTINE

    What was so important?

MADONNA

    I want you to keep an open mind.

    I want you to keep your mouth shut.

VALENTINE

    What?

MADONNA

    I'm serious.

    I will never be more serious.

5—Int. Basement steps

They are walking into the basement. Bending not to bang his head. One single light bulb behind them.

VALENTINE

    You want me to move something?

6—*Madonna goes to the back wall of typical cluttered basement shelves. She is reaching into them.*

7—Valentine squints. What is this?

8—Madonna has grabbed the hidden clasp on the back wall.

9—She pulls the clasp and reveals that the shelf wall is actually a door that opens. It reveals itself to be a door.

10—A door to another room that Valentine, although he's lived here his entire life, did not know was there.

VALENTINE (CONT'D)
Since when is this a door?

I lived in this house eighteen years . . .

MADONNA
It was your father's panic room.

A safe room. In case something happened.

11—Before they go inside, the light coming from inside the mystery room, she turns around and says to him.

VALENTINE
Ma, you're freakin' me out.

MADONNA
I would never put you in this position if I didn't think you were ready.

And I meant what I said: Listen. Don't talk.

Do you trust me?

12—Same but tighter. He has no idea what is going on. She wants his full attention.

VALENTINE
What—the—fuck, Ma?

MADONNA
Don't make me slap those terrible words out of your mouth.

VALENTINE
Seriously, what is going on?

13—Over Valentine's shoulder. She gives him one last look as she is about to open the door.

PAGE 38

1—Big panel. She opens the door, and a handsome man and woman in cheap suits with coffee are just standing to greet him. Clearly they are FBI. Their names are AGENT GLASS and AGENT BELL.

It is a very well-lit, clean white room. With a table and a couple of chairs. And some coffee. That is it.

In the corner we can see there is a monitor that may have been hooked up to some kind of panic room system that has long been outdated.

AGENT GLASS

    Valentine Gallo, it is a pleasure to meet you.

2—Valentine cautiously enters the room at his mother's gesture as she closes the door. There is something very odd and alien about this white, well-lit, clean room.

VALENTINE

    The fuck is this?

    Do you live in this room?

AGENT GLASS

    This is a place where we can talk and be sure that
    no one is listening.

VALENTINE

    Who would be listening in our kitchen?

3—Valentine looks at his mom and can't for the life of him figure out what this is about. She is trying to keep him calm but with a mother's stern, strong demeanor.

MADONNA

    Did I say just sit down and listen?

    I said to sit down and listen!

VALENTINE

    I'll sit down when you tell me what the hell this is.

4—Over Valentine's shoulder. The agents both know that what they are saying are words that have never been spoken aloud. And once they are said out loud . . . they can never be taken back.

AGENT GLASS

    We're federal agents, Mr. Gallo.

AGENT BELL

    From outside the territories.

AGENT GLASS

    Obviously.

5—Valentine looks at his mother like she is announcing she is an alien from outer space.

MADONNA

    And so am I.

PAGE 39

1—The agents lean in and don't give him a second to digest that whopper.

AGENT BELL

The families have had their run of things on the East Coast for so many years . . .

I'm not sure you even know there was a time when what they do was considered illegal.

2—Valentine steps back without even realizing he's doing it as the agents and his mother talk among themselves. His back is almost to the closed door.

MADONNA

He's not stupid.

AGENT BELL

It's just people his age—

MADONNA

How old are YOU?

This is the way it's been since before ALL OF US was born . . . shut the fuck up.

VALENTINE

Ma?

3—Over Valentine's shoulder. His mother sits down and we can feel like a huge weight is being lifted off of her as she says these words she has been dying to say to him for so many years.

MADONNA

This isn't how it's supposed to be, Val.

OK?

The families, the territories . . .

They—it ain't right.

VALENTINE

It's—it's the way it is.

MADONNA

But that don't make it right.

4—Valentine is appropriately frustrated.

VALENTINE

What the fuck are you talking about??!!

You just went to my ceremony!! I'm sworn in by blood!!

5—*Madonna looks right at him and says her ultimate truth.*

MADONNA

And you were BORN an undercover federal agent.

6—*Slightly low looking up. Valentine knows that his mother is not joking.*

PAGE 40

1—*Over Valentine's shoulder. She is looking right at him and telling him how it is.*

MADONNA (CONT'D)

I birthed you into this world for this purpose.

No outsider could ever infiltrate the families.

It had to be blood.

It had to be one of us.

2—*Same but tighter. She explains it as clearly as she can.*

MADONNA (CONT'D)

They killed your father and your father's father.

They killed them, Val.

No one pays. No one goes to jail.

They just get richer and richer.

So I BIRTHED you into this.

3—*Valentine is open-mouthed shocked. This is fucking real??*

MADONNA (CONT'D)

All the while praying that this day would never need to come.

That somehow the world would right itself.

But that day never came.

And here we are.

4—*Madonna looks at him and says this with complete confidence.*

MADONNA (CONT'D)

You're going to pull this all apart, Val.

All of it.

Every single brick. From the inside.

And they'll never even see it coming.

5—*The agents are very excited but trying to keep their composure.*

AGENT BELL

    Do you know what the families did to take control of this part of the country?

AGENT GLASS

    Does he know who his great-grandfather was?

6—*Madonna stops talking. She looks right at her son. She means business. But this secret will floor him.*

MADONNA

    No.

7—*Valentine looks back at her. He is scared to ask??*

PAGE 41

Full-page spread

Ext. The East Coast—sunset

The sun sets across the Eastern Seaboard.

The sun sets across the United States of Murder Incorporated.

Small white typewriter text across the middle of the spread reads: The United States of Murder Incorporated.